AF153994

Lilia Ames

Are you Cheerless?

SALZWASSER
VERLAG

Lilia Ames

Are you Cheerless?

Reprint of the original, first published in 1859.

1st Edition 2022 | ISBN: 978-3-37512-378-9

Verlag (Publisher): Salzwasser Verlag GmbH, Zeilweg 44, 60439 Frankfurt, Deutschland
Vertretungsberechtigt (Authorized to represent): E. Roepke, Zeilweg 44, 60439 Frankfurt, Deutschland
Druck (Print): Books on Demand GmbH, In de Tarpen 42, 22848 Norderstedt, Deutschland

ARE YOU CHEERLESS?

ARE YOU CHEERLESS?

BY

LILIA AMES.

LONDON:

JAMES NISBET & CO., BERNERS STREET.

1859.

CONTENTS.

j

CHAPTER II.

THE BALM OF GILEAD.

AND now, dear sir, let me address you with the tenderest sympathy, and let us search and see if we can find anything to arouse and comfort your drooping spirit.

Does no one love you or care for your comfort? Are you looked upon, or accustomed to look upon yourself as a useless ruin, which would be better cleared away?

As you sat on that bench, in the sunshine, did not even your poor, chilly frame feel its pleasant influence? As

your languid eye took a rapid survey
of the scene, did it not seem beautiful
and happy? Is not creation glorious?
You will say, "It may be so, but
what is that to *me?* I cannot enjoy it,
and it rather adds to my misery to see
all so bright and active." But pause,
dear sir, for a little while, to reflect
that this earth was not made for a
gloomy prison-house; fallen as it is
from its original beauty, it bears the
marks of supreme love throughout every
part of it. Yes, it is the handiwork of
Divine Love, and, as such, should soften,
warm, and cheer even your heart. You
will say: "Look at me, and tell me if
love caused this ruin?"

I am not going to enter into the
veiled subject of why God allowed sin,

and consequently sorrow, sickness, and
death to enter this beautiful world and
mar his creatures, but I can confidently
answer—yes; I can assert that *love*
can, out of everything—out of this very
heavy affliction, which oppresses your
body and hangs heavy on your mind—
draw the sweetest fruit and the most
enduring happiness.

Probably you scarcely ever read.
Politics are distasteful to you—you
have done with them; travels only tan-
talize you, in your present state of
mind, by depicting scenes you can
never again enjoy; works of fiction
have lost their relish, or only mock
your heart with pictures of ideal beauty
and pleasures passed from you long
years ago.

Your Bible is most distasteful of all.
The style, language, and subjects are
alike foreign to your tastes and wishes;
yet sometimes you cast a melancholy
glance towards it, as a thought it must
be had recourse to some day or other
passes through your mind; but that
day *never comes*, and there remains the
neglected Bible. Perhaps you would not
confess as much plainly, but you would
much rather sit listlessly gazing into
the fire, or indulging in the gloomiest
views of the past, present, and future,
than take up that Bible for half an
hour's perusal. Yet, dear sir, that
neglected book, studied in simple faith,
can show you *all that your heart and
soul* need most at this moment, can
light up your dull eyes, smooth that

careworn brow, shed a radiance over that sad countenance, fill your breast with joy, and your life with peace.

Do not throw aside my little book, and say, "this is fanaticism;" only read it through, I beseech you, before you condemn my poor efforts.

You are most forlorn and sad. You have tried doctors and systems till you are tired of them all; you remain the same. Well then, I conjure you, by all that is valuable in the present world and the world to come, to try my prescription, to taste and see whether the "balm of Jesus" contains any properties you have vainly sought elsewhere.

You are weary of all things; your whole existence is a weariness; you

are heavy-laden with sickness, desolate-
ness, and (though you know not its
extent) with *sin*. Do not, dear sir,
turn aside in distaste. *Sin* is the root
and cause of all your trouble. Sin
brought sickness, old age, and all affliction into the world. It is sin which
spreads a thick veil between you and
your God, which hides from your eyes
all those things which could give you
solid peace, which gives you a repug-
nance to the blessed Scriptures, and
makes you almost angrily turn your
back on heavenly subjects. This bitter
enemy is keeping back from you the
Bread of Life, the Light of the World,
the Comforter, the Physician, the pre-
vailing Advocate, the "Friend that
sticketh closer than a brother," the

B

Shepherd who can lead you into green pastures, the Redeemer who shed His own blood to purchase eternal life for you, and who is *at this moment* ready to take the burden of all your sins and sorrows upon Himself, and give you, in exchange, the spotless robe of His righteousness. Jesus Christ, the Saviour of the world, Satan would hide from you, and I earnestly call upon you *now* to receive Him into your heart. Open your Bible. Turn to the 11th Matthew, 28th, 29th, and 30th verses:

" Come unto Me all ye that labour and are heavy laden, and I will give you rest. Take my yoke upon you, and learn of me; for I am meek and lowly in heart; and ye shall find rest unto your souls.

" For my yoke is easy, and my burden is light."

Mark well those words :

" My yoke is easy, and my burden is light." And now, dear sir, put down the book, and reflect on this blessed portion of God's word, " Come unto Me."

You may say: " How am I to come?" I will quote some lines of a well-known hymn :—

" Just as I am, without one plea—
But that Thy blood was shed for me,
And that Thou bidst me come to Thee.
O Lamb of God, I come!

" Just as I am, and waiting not
To rid my soul of one dark blot,
To Thee whose blood can cleanse each spot.
O Lamb of God, I come!"

This is the *spirit* in which to come.

Blessed privilege! "*Just as I am.*" No preparation, but a humble heart like the publican in the parable, who smote on his breast, and presumed not even to raise his eyes to heaven.

You feel, perhaps, your heart like a stone. But it *must* not remain so, or you are lost for ever, and cut off from all hope here and hereafter. May I beseech you to say continually to Jesus, "Lord, *take* my heart, I cannot give it thee;" and, in His own time, He will take it, having subdued it by love, into His own keeping.

Say: "Cleanse the thoughts of my heart by the inspiration of thy Holy Spirit, that I may perfectly love thee, and worthily magnify thy holy name," and His love will soon purify your heart, and *constrain* you to magnify His name. Lay all the heavy weight of your sorrow, your sickness, your desolation, at the foot of Christ's cross, and you will find rest; such a sweet calm will enter into your soul; Jesus will become all in all to you. He will then speak plainly to you in the promises richly scattered through the Bible. He will then support, comfort, strengthen and sympathize with you, and you will know the peace of God, which passeth all understanding.

Study your Saviour's life and sayings—always with prayer for the Holy Spirit to open the eyes of your understanding—and then you will be easily drawn to take upon you his yoke, and to kneel low at his footstool.

The service of the world has been hard upon you, and whatever short-lived pleasure it may have given you, it has left you now hopeless and desolate. Do, dear sir! I beseech you try the yoke of Christ, for just where the world most turns its back Christ is most full of all you need, and most near to your helplessness, if you will put away your garment of pride and be clothed with humility. Jesus will teach you all he requires you to know; He is meek and lowly, and, if you give yourself to Him, He will deal so wisely and tenderly with you!

You will, indeed, find His service perfect freedom. You will then feel ennobled as well as comforted, because you will feel that God the Father loves you, and has drawn you to Christ, the appointed way to glory. You will feel that Christ is interceding daily and hourly for you, and is enfolding you in His own spirit. You will feel the motions of that blessed spirit, that spirit of unutterable peace, and purity, and joy — you will feel them within your own soul, urging you to thanksgiving, and you will believe that ministering angels are sent to watch over you, and to ward off evil from an heir of salvation. Will not your poor, oppressed heart rise at these thoughts? Will you not try to attain this state?

But you may say, "I have been grovelling all my life in sensuality, and now that I am worn out can *I* hope ever to be what you describe?" Yes, dear sir, you can. Read in the sixty-eighth Psalm: "Though ye have lien among the pots, yet shall ye be as the wings of a dove covered with silver, and her feathers with yellow gold."

Is not that cheering, encouraging, and gracious? You may say: "All this sounds very well; but I have no good desires, no power to move towards God, no reason why I should expect Him to look upon me with anything but anger; I have turned my back on Him all my life."

In reading what I have written have you heaved an involuntary sigh? That sigh was a desire after something good. Have you felt the faintest wish to be what I have feebly depicted? That faint wish was a going-out of your soul to meet Christ.

Cherish that wish; dwell on it; hold it up to God to be nourished and strengthened, and it will leaven your whole being, and you will become a new creature.

Listen to the voice of your neglected and outraged Maker:—

"O Israel, thou hast destroyed thyself; but in Me is thine help."—Hosea, xiii.

When you receive these wondrous words, look up to Jesus, and say :—

"Lord, save me, I perish !"

You *must* not—you *dare* not—remain as you are :

"Break up your fallow ground: for it is time to seek the Lord, till he come and rain righteousness upon you."—Hosea, x.

Go, dear sir, and sit under the shadow of the cross: that is seeking the Lord. Say, "Be merciful to me a sinner:" that is the best prayer. Ask Jesus to cleanse your soul in that precious blood which flowed for you: that is what will make you pure in the eyes of God; for He will then look upon you as clothed in the spotless robe of His well-beloved Son's righteousness, and you will be accepted, justified, freely forgiven, for Jesus' sake.

Then, dear sir, you will know the joy of sin forgiven, of the favour of God instead of his frown; then will you, in your sickness and helplessness, be able to say: "My flesh and my heart faileth: but God is the strength of my heart, and my portion for ever."—

Ps. lxxiii. Then you will know what it is to be *born again*, an expression which perhaps you have hitherto ridiculed or despised. You will feel a new life within your now cheerless heart; an internal vigour—a joy—a *breathing* of the Spirit of God, which will make you aspire to do something for His service. "Do something for God?" you may exclaim; "in my poor helpless condition?"

Yes, dear sir, even were you laid prostrate on your bed, and could move neither hand or foot, you could honour and glorify God by believing in His Son. You know what the thief on the Cross did. He turned in strong faith, as a dying man and a perishing sinner, to the Saviour of sinners. He thus

honoured God, and was accepted. Can
you be more helpless, more sinful, than
that thief? You are old, and have
done nothing all your life for God. I
acknowledge that it *is* the eleventh hour
with you, but your Saviour calls you
now to come into His vineyard, and
will reward you even as the labourers
who have borne the burden and heat of
the day.

God gave you leisure, perhaps health,
certainly once youth, health, opportu-
nities. You have wasted and misused
them all. Perhaps you owe your Master even ten thousand talents. What
is to be done? You have nothing,
absolutely *nothing* to offer Him in pay-
ment. *What is to be done?* Kneel before God; ask Him, in simple faith, to

have pity on your extremity, for *Jesus'*
sake, and He will freely forgive you all
that debt. The gratitude of your soul
for such amazing mercy will prepare it
to receive that Holy Spirit, proceeding
from the Father and the Son, that Lord
and Giver of life, who will take up His
abode in your now cold, empty heart,
and beam out in your now dejected
countenance.

Then will the *fruits* of the Spirit
gradually develop themselves in you,
and make of the wilderness a watered
garden.

Turn, dear sir, to the fifth chapter of
Galatians, and consider these fruits as
there enumerated. First, *Love.*

Perhaps you sometimes feel that no-
body loves you, that you are unlove-

able. Oh! do not think so! Your
Heavenly Father loves you; the Redeemer, who died on the Cross for
your soul, loves you; the pure Holy
Spirit loves you; the ministering angels
love you; all God's people on earth are
ready to welcome and love you, and
long and yearn, as I do, to benefit and
comfort you; so that you *are* beloved
and cared for, *just as you are.*

The Spirit can produce a responsive
love in *your* bosom. A fountain of pure
love can spring up in your heart, and
the Bible would reveal to you its deep
treasures of *everlasting* love, and feed
that fountain with its tender consola-
tions, its unspeakably gracious promises,
its gentle upbraidings, its mercy even
to the uttermost. Then love would con-

strain you to say: "What shall I render unto the Lord for all His benefits." And the holy prompter within would soon point out to you many ways in which you may evince your love to your Heavenly Benefactor.

Joy is the next fruit.

More or less, every child of God must feel joy when he thinks of his guilt washed away in the blood of the Lamb, of the everlasting arms which are under him, of the strength which shall be made perfect in His weakness, of the perfect righteousness of Christ which is imputed to him, of the light which shall ever shine upon his path here, and conduct him even through the valley of the shadow of death, and of the eternity of happiness he will re-

ceive, as a free gift, free from age, sickness, weariness, partings, and, above
all, *sin*.

That joy will be a staff when the
spirit is faint, for "The joy of the Lord
is your strength."

Then comes that pleasant word
Peace.

Peace with your reconciled God;
peace with your once accusing con-
science; peace with all the world.
"The peace of God which passeth ún-
derstanding." The gloomy, foggy day,
the long winter evening, the sleepless
night, the often-recurring weariness of
debility, the paroxysm of pain, may re-
turn as they have done of yore, but
they will no longer be writhed under
with rebellious and impotent temper, or

fretted at with restless discontent; they
will not be pleasant, but you will remember that not a sparrow can fall to
the ground without divine permission,
and that He who has numbered the
very hairs of your head permits all
these trials that you may be more and
more freed from the dross which has
dimmed the fine gold. Peace will pre-
vail, and inconceivably lighten the load
of inevitable suffering.

Long-suffering.

This is, perhaps, dear sir, very foreign
to your frame of mind, which may be
testy and irritable. But the Spirit can
change all this, and can turn your
thoughts to the *ten thousand talents* forgiven you, can remind you of the high
privileges to which a child of God is

c

admitted, and of the wondrous fact
that the great Shepherd is not ashamed
to own you and cherish you; and lo,
the evil temper would flee away, and
you would bear, without one murmur,
all that you were called to endure.
You would experience the feelings
which caused the great Apostle to exclaim:

"For I reckon that the sufferings of
this present time are not worthy to be
compared with the glory which shall be
revealed in us."—Romans viii.

Yes, dear sir, only turn to Christ,
only accept His offered salvation, only
crave His spirit, and I can confidently
encircle you with this text, whilst you
suffer in the flesh:

"And we know that all things work

together for good to them that love God, to them who are the called according to His purpose."—Romans viii.

Give long-suffering a place in your heart, and then the awkwardness or neglect of a servant, which now shakes your feeble frame with anger, would only call forth a mild rebuke, far more touching and efficacious than the fiercest wrath. The resignation expressed in your words and looks to God's will would also honour Him and edify all who witnessed it, so that, if not actually won over to the Saviour who has thus changed *you*, at least they would strive to give you their best service—the service of affection, for then you would be *loved*, because the image of your Maker would be returning to you.

Gentleness.

Our evil tempers, if unchained, tear us to pieces, as the bird destroys her strength by vainly beating herself against the wires of her cage. By giving way to violent emotions or peevish humours, you not only quench pity and affection in those around you, but you render yourself more supremely wretched, and feel at enmity with heaven and earth. But the gentleness which springs from the indwelling of Christ's Holy Spirit both soothes and heals, and I am convinced that your ailments would lose nearly half their virulence if borne with bowed submission and gentle acquiescence to the will of God. " Thy will be done" is an exorcism of the most powerful efficacy to scare away the evil passions of rebellion and wrath, and bring heavenly balm into our hearts !

Then, dear sir, pray and strive to possess that spirit of gentleness; and may God be very gracious to you, and help you mightily to conquer all the perverseness of your nature.

Goodness.

Washed white in the blood of the Lamb, inhabited by the holy dove of God, the language of your heart being continually, " Lord, what wouldest thou have me to do?" — "Speak, Lord, thy servant heareth," how can anything else than goodness be the result ? Not *your* goodness, but the goodness of the indwelling spirit. You will be good in the sight of the Father,

who will look upon you as a member of
Christ, and, as such, be well pleased
with you. Goodness will be the delibe-
rate choice of your renewed will; what
was once bitter will now be sweet,
and in *everything* you will have your
eyes opened to see the goodness of the
great Creator, even in your own failing
frame, as recollecting that, by all this
suffering, your precious soul is being
refined and purified, *though as by fire*,
in order that, *soul and body*, you may be
ready in the end to enter into the joy of
your Lord. Goodness, springing from
such a source, does, indeed, irradiate the
most unlovely features, and beam forth
upon all who see it as evidently *not of
earth*. It is independent of all external
circumstances, for I have seen it in the

hospital, on the bed of languishing sickness, and in the home of cold poverty.

Faith.

This is the highest, most strengthening, most comforting fruit of the Spirit. Faith conquers everything; faith makes you forget your poor self— all your sins, your sorrows, your sickness, your wretchedness — and fixes your eyes and heart on the once crucified, now glorified, Saviour, who is your advocate with the Father, and through whose intercession it is that that dreadful sentence, " Cut him down, why cumbereth he the ground," has not been executed upon you long ago.

You will see, by the eye of faith, your sins nailed to the cross of Christ, and your salvation completed when that blessed head bowed in death. Yes, dear sir, if your place is at the foot of that cross, if you are saying, in earnest desire, "Lord, I believe, help thou mine unbelief," you are a saved soul, and faith will open to your rejoicing view all the riches you possess in possessing Jesus, and a sweet serenity will diffuse itself through your mind as you lean on the Rock of Ages. Though the storm may be around, Jesus will be in the ship.

Meekness.

I have little doubt that you have been accustomed to view meekness as a mean, pitiful state of mind, very well, perhaps, in women, but wholly incompatible with manly spirit. But, alas! dear sir, when wheeled about helplessly in your invalid chair, —

when lifted from it, and leaning trem-
blingly on the arm of any one who
may be hired to support you,—where
is pride? What avails chafing and
swelling against the inevitable? What
avails struggling like a bull in a net,
or, still worse, sinking into sullen de-
spair? Oh, no, believe me, meekness
is not a mean feeling, it springs from
the highest, noblest sources. When
did Jesus, the Son of God, appear more
Godlike than when, the very personifi-
cation of meekness, he stood in the
judgment-hall, calm and silent, grand
in his humility? And when did his
proud enemies and accusers appear
more base and contemptible as they
stood there in strong contrast to their
divine prisoner?

Meekness is as soul-subduing **and** loveable as it is noble. When did Jesus appear more winning and irresistible than when he proclaimed himself "meek and lowly," and invited us all to come and learn to be such from him?

Meekness is a peace-giving, enduring grace, when grafted by Christ's holy spirit into the heart of man, and enriches the warrior and the statesman as much as it adorns the frail, delicate woman. Believe me, it could smooth your pillow in many a long night, lull your pain through many a weary day, and render you a fit recipient for many a comforting season of communion from heaven.

Temperance.

You may say, " Without a shadow of

appetite, or the power of joining in any amusement, it is mockery to talk to *me* of temperance."

Your appetite may be sickly, but may you not render it still more so by forcing nature to receive what she would reject, and what is poison to her debilitated powers? Perhaps you have a passing fancy to an indigestible or highly-seasoned dish, and your ample means enable you to gratify all your fancies. You swallow some hasty morsels, put the rest distastefully away, perhaps, with ruffled temper, accusing the cook or tradesman of carelessness. The digestion, in its extremely weak state, is sorely tried, and fails in the trial put upon it, and the irritation of mind makes matters worse, so that each meal

increases the mischief, instead of nourish-
ing the frame.

Might it not be worth your while to
try the simplest, lightest food, in small
quantities, according to your appetite;
above all, before you taste it, asking
Jesus to bless it to your nourishment,
and to make you thankful for His kind
provision; and, after every repast, to
say, from your heart, " Thank God for
what I have received?" This would
produce serenity of mind, and serenity
is the perfection of temperance. Your
body would repose with your mind,
and thus you would have a far better
chance of being refreshed by your food.

Then that general temperance of a
well-regulated mind, which the Holy
Spirit alone can bring about,—turning

wild, miserable confusion, into order, —would be more beneficial to you than all the tonics or elixirs the world can offer, though they are valuable in their place, and with God's blessing.

Dear sir, I *do* feel for you. I breathed a heartfelt petition that sunny day on which I first saw you, that Christ would take you into His tender keeping. I acknowledge, with deep sympathy, that your case is very afflictive, to be so weak and helpless, and the dejection of your countenance touched me to the soul. I am an unknown friend, I trust sent by Jesus, to give you *some* comfort; and, in much weakness, but entire dependence on His blessing, I am trying to lead you to the fountain of all blessings.

The cloud is around you, and over you, but *do* try and meditate on that precious text which once aroused me from deep and rebellious grief:

"And it shall come to pass, when I bring a cloud over the earth, that the bow shall be seen in the cloud."— Genesis ix.

Jesus is the bow you must look to; and, if you will search the Scriptures, you will trace this bow all through the Old Testament, breaking out, every now and then, in clear prophecies or tender promises and invitations, till it is seen steadily shining in the New Testament, filling the humble, waiting heart with that sweetest of cordials— hope.

Dear sir, let the language of your

soul be: "Thy will be done!"—and it *will* be done. *His will* is your present peace and your everlasting happiness. When 1 looked into your cheerless eyes, their language plainly was: "Who will show me any good?" God grant that it may now be: "Lord, lift Thou up the light of Thy countenance upon me!"

He will not turn a deaf ear to the cry of the poor and needy supplicant, but He will be your shield, whilst you remain on earth, saving you from all the darts of the Wicked One, who seeks to destroy you,—blunting the sharp edge of all pain and trial, and, finally, He will be your everlasting, your "exceeding great reward"—in Heaven.

CHAPTER III.

THE ALL IN ALL.

AND now, dear sir, supposing that Jesus has revealed Himself to your soul, and that you have turned to Him in sincerity, allow me to offer you a few hints as to how I think you might pass portions of your time pleasantly and profitably.

When first you awake, lift up your heart to God, and say: "Bless me, O my Father, for Jesus' sake!"

I would advise you to rise as early as your infirmities will permit, as I think remaining in bed, unless absolutely necessary, and ordered by the physicians, tends to deaden the spirit throughout the day.

When you are dressed, I would have you, as long as you can bend the knee, to kneel before the Lord your Maker, and say, *every morning :* " Father, give me Thy Holy Spirit, in all things to direct and rule my heart, for Jesus' sake."

Before your light and simple breakfast, were it only a cup of tea, and as long as you are able to read, I would have you assemble your servants, or even one servant, and read a few verses of Scripture to them, followed by a collect or short prayer, ending with the Lord's Prayer.

This may seem very irksome at first,

D

but how can you feel easy if you utterly neglect the spiritual welfare of your domestics? Or how can you expect faithfulness and integrity in their services to you?

Then your own little repast must not be taken till you have asked a blessing on it. This constant communion with Jesus will become *so* precious to you in time—to *lean on Him* in everything.

As soon after breakfast as convenient (but certainly before you begin the occupations of the day), a certain portion of your time should be devoted to prayer and meditation; and I would earnestly entreat you to *fix* that time, and to let nothing put you off it. I warn you that the active enemy of your soul will try to render this communion with your own heart, and with God, more difficult, or distasteful, or inconvenient than any other thing you may attempt. And why? Because he well knows the precious fruit it will bear, and the strength which you will gain, day by day, against him and his assaults. I would advise you to read your Bible *carefully* through—even a chapter at a time—and, as you read, to mark with a pencil such texts as *come home* to you with power. Then take one of these texts every morning, at the time of your daily meditation, *and put it into your heart.* By degrees you will become rich in the Scriptures, and in times of need these precious texts will rise up to guide, or warn, or strengthen, or comfort you.

I would, then, have you simply and heartily to tell Jesus what you want, always placing your spiritual wants first, and beginning by praising and thanking God for all his mercies.

You want to sit at the feet of Jesus, to be enfolded in His spirit, to be gently dealt with, to have a patient soul, to be strong in duty, to be wholly guided by his counsel, to have Him to take care of all your concerns, and to sprinkle your soul every day with the blood of atonement, which alone can remove the stains daily contracted by sin. Your own heart will soon supply you with subjects to bring before that bounteous and gracious Saviour, who is

more ready to hear than you to pray.
I especially direct your attention to the
Collects in our Book of Common Prayer,
as the most perfect and comprehensive
forms of *written* petition that uninspired
writers ever penned. I am convinced
that the more you advance in the spiritual life, the more will your heart
and judgment adopt them, and, once
familiar to you, they would often come
unbidden to your memory, in times
when they exactly express your wants.

For meditation I would have you
read a text or chapter, and then, look-
ing up for God's help, lay down your
open Bible and reflect on it. What I
mean by *meditation* is, first, to consider
the portion in question just as it stands
—*literally ;* then to compare yourself,

your state and desires by it; then to
pray that you may attain what it en-
joins, or typifies or promises, as you are
led to see all its hidden meaning, in an
implied precept, a foreshadowing of
Jesus, or a blessing ready to be bestowed
on the humble disciple.

You would thus discover mines of
wealth in that Holy Book, which the
longest life would fail to exhaust; and
remember, dear sir, that meditation is
the very food and nourishment of your
soul. Starve your soul, and it grows
cold and dead; feed it bounteously with
this manna, and it will grow rapidly in
strength and brightness. The weakness
of your body may prevent you doing
all that I have sketched at one time,
but I am merely suggesting what *I*

have found a most profitable course; and that adorable Redeemer, who so tenderly felt for our infirmities, and who said with such ineffable compassion, "The spirit, indeed, is willing, but the flesh is weak," will accept your *will*, will accept the heavenward look, the penitent sigh, even the rising wish, which may be all your languor allows, and will count them as precious things, if offered at the foot of the cross.

As long as you are able to be drawn about in your chair, through the open air, I trust that you will go out, and, with a renewed heart, you will look very differently from what you once did on all things around you, and each beauty in creation will attract your

attention, and often will your bosom
swell with love and gratitude towards
the Maker and Benefactor who has
left us so much to delight us in this
sin-marred world, and has promised
to us who love Him a *new earth*, beautiful and perfect, wherein we shall rejoice
with joy unspeakable, and wherein
dwelleth righteousness. Yes, dear sir,
only let me imagine you with a heart
in Jesus' keeping, and never, never
again would that hopeless dejection,
which, to witness, drew the tears into
my eyes, again overcloud your countenance and bow your head. If you
can hold a pen, I think you would find
it very interesting to note down daily
some little record of your feelings or
progress, or mercy received, or even

some text which comforts you, in a sort of journal, and reading it over occasionally, would be profitable and pleasant. Indeed it is the absolute duty of every Christian, either with tongue or pen, to tell what great things God has done for his soul, and even how bounteously He has dealt with him in temporal matters.

Only imagine, dear sir, if, in addition to what you now suffer, you had stern poverty to contend with; cold drafts of air blowing through the ill-secured room on your delicate frame; no fire, or scanty covering, whilst you shivered through the severe winter; coarse food, unfitted for your poor state of health, and no attendance, except what occasional kindness volunteered. Consider what *might have been* and *what is ;* and thank God, either by tongue or pen, for all his goodness.

Such is the *vital* power of true religion, that with all the discomforts I have enumerated as attendant on extreme poverty, I have seen the countenance radiant, and heard the language of thanksgiving.

With regard to reading—even supposing you able to do so—I am afraid to recommend any books, not knowing your tastes, or peculiarities of thought. But one thing I will say, that I should prefer your *not* reading *any* Commentaries on the Bible. The Holy Spirit opened *my* eyes and understanding to see and receive the riches of God's word; and if you always ask His help, when you take up that holy book, He will teach you far, far better than all human comment, and *He* cannot err.

There are many points on which you may feel desirous of conversing with some more experienced Christian, and a *really* pious friend is sometimes a great comfort. Have you never met a sincere Christian, or heard of such a one in your former circle of acquaintance? Perhaps he may have been scorned and avoided by you in your days of pride. If there should be such a man, to whom you could send or write, though he may be a perfect stranger to you, he will come to you immediately (for all Christians love one another), rejoiced that he is privileged to do anything for his God; and what task so delightful to him as

that of assisting a returning prodigal,
or a stray sheep, to his father's home,
to his shepherd's fold?

Such a man will come into your
chamber with "airs from heaven" about
him; and as he depends entirely on
the Holy Spirit to give him a tongue
and wisdom, he will be able to throw a
light on many passages of Scripture
which may puzzle or trouble you; be-
sides which, he, like his Master, will
be full of sympathy, meekness, and
gentleness, and you will see in his
countenance a serene cheerfulness which
will do your inmost heart good, like a
cordial.

You need not fear anything stern or
dictatorial in such a man; and what
you once called "*Cant*," will be to

your soul like "the small rain upon the tender herb."

If to speak of redeeming love, of free grace, of a reconciled Father, of the commuted sentence, of the full pardon, of the perfect freedom of God's service, of the support in the last hour, and the everlasting happiness,—if this be *cant*, God grant *me* such, by whatever name it may be called, both in life and death.

You may again say: "In *my* state, what can I *do* for God?"

If Christ is in your heart, you will be shown in what way you can serve God. Remember what the poet says:—

" Who does the best his circumstance allows,
  Does well, acts nobly; angels could no more."

And as Milton so beautifully remarks:—

" They also serve who only stand and wait."

It is the *attitude* of your mind that God will look to; the readiness of the will, the meek acquiescence in all his appointments. This is the best work; and if active work is needed, He can find it for you, and strengthen you to do it. The change wrought in your whole conduct and appearance will of itself testify to those around you that something heavenly has been at work, and, as you gain mental strength and courage, many a word spoken in season, —an expression of gratitude for God's mercies, a patient "God's will be done!" a text pointed out for the benefit of another,—will honour God. With regard to public charities, whatever you are disposed to give,—I would recommend you to procure a little book called "The

Charities of London," by Sampson Low, and then you can select for yourself,— and whenever you *give*, I would urge you to ask Jesus to accept and bless it, remembering those gracious words—"He that hath pity upon the poor, lendeth unto the Lord: and look, what he layeth out, it shall be paid him again."

What an incitement! "*Lendeth unto the Lord.*" And it *will* be paid you again a thousandfold, in the delight you will feel in giving, and the accumulation of your treasure in heaven. But, after all, the most acceptable gift to God is *yourself*. Give your body, soul, and spirit to Christ; ask him to *take* them, —I know that you cannot even *give* them in your own strength,—and your heart is the most costly gift you can

make him for all he has done for you,—
and then your duties will be made plain,
your path light, and you will be the
free and happy servant of the best and
wisest Master.

I am aware, dear sir, that in your
state of health there will be seasons of
dejection, when the body will drag down
the mind. In such seasons, perhaps the
most comfortable text of Scripture will
fail to warm your heart, the most precious promise be insufficient to cheer
you; but *then*, in the dark hour, you
can lay your poor weak head at the foot
of the cross, as a sick, weary child would
repose his on the bosom of his mother,
and stay quietly there till the light
breaks again.

" Who is among you that feareth the

Lord, that obeyeth the voice of His servant, that walketh in darkness and hath no light? Let him trust in the name of the Lord, and stay upon his God."—Isaiah l.

Sometimes, in these seasons, you may be tempted to think that you are not forgiven fully, freely,—that the hope is a delusion,—that you have no right to rejoice. If so tempted, try to fix your mind on the recorded truth, that Jesus came from Heaven, lived, suffered, and died, for the express purpose of working out a complete salvation for such as you,—a finished righteousness for such as you, who have no righteousness of your own;— that He bore the whole weight and punishment of guilty creatures, such

E

as you, who *must* otherwise perish,—
who endured the penalty of death,
under bodily and spiritual agony such
as *we* cannot imagine,—in order that
death might have no sting for such as
you. Thus does He not only free you
from all guilt, but opens heaven freely
to your soul, your ransomed, blood-
bought soul, and ask you simply to
accept this great salvation. Try to
combat all tempting doubts with such
reflections.

Whatever sceptics may say to the
contrary, *this* faith, this belief in *free
grace*, is the only purifier of the heart
of man. This faith, believe me, dear
sir, is the only really substantial pos-
session you can have; all that you
actually see and grasp here is a shadow,

because it passeth away; but the things which belong to God shall never pass away, and no man can take them from you—no man, by force or guile, can take from you the treasure which, I earnestly trust, you will begin this day to lay up for yourself in Heaven.

CHAPTER IV.

VICTORY!

THERE is the last great trial—death—
which perhaps you have been fighting
against for years, and look upon with
infinite dread. I do not deny its terror
and solemnity, and, in an unconverted
state, no pen could exaggerate its fear-
fulness. But I would have you store
up provision against that hour of need.
I would advise you to set apart some
time every week especially to consider
this period, and to examine yourself in
reference to it. Above all, consider
whether you are resting *wholly* on

Christ's merit and Christ's atonement
for acceptance with God. The best cry
to gain admittance to Heaven in that
hour is: "None but Christ—nothing
but Christ!" Yes, poor sinner, this
cry can open Heaven to you, and your
trembling spirit will not wander about
a stranger when it leaves your body.
Christ, your elder brother, who actually
exists in human, though glorified flesh,
and once actually lived amongst men,
will be at hand to receive your soul. If
your faith rests on the Rock of free
grace, you may repeat to yourself, with
humble confidence: "Absent from the
body, present with the Lord." Lay up
in your memory, from time to time,
such texts as may most avail in the
dying hour, such as: "The blood of

Jesus Christ cleanseth from all sin;"
"Though your sins be as scarlet, they
shall be as white as snow;" "Lo, I am
with you always."

Strive now, whilst you have time
allowed you, to found your hope on
the Rock of Ages, and then, in that
solemn hour, we may humbly trust,
that Rock will not fail you. The
everlasting arms will be under you.
If, like Peter on the sea, you should
begin to sink, the face of redeeming love will be over you if you
have strength to look up to it, and
though now your poor heart is sad and
your frame weary and painful, you shall
be received into that place where there
is *fulness* of joy and pleasures for ever-
more.

And now, dear sir, I bid you an affectionate and earnest farewell. We shall, in all probability, never meet on earth, but we *certainly shall meet again* in the great day when our Saviour shall come to judge the world. You and I must both stand before the judgment-seat of Christ. How am I to meet you?

Am I to hear those dreadful words pronounced upon you:

"Depart from me, ye cursed, into everlasting fire, prepared for the devil and his angels?"—or am I to welcome you with unspeakable joy, and, both of us clothed in the wedding garment of Christ's righteousness, shall we enter into the joy of our Lord? And shall it be said of us:

"These are they which came out of great tribulation, and have washed their robes, and made them white in the blood of the Lamb?"

Jack & Evans, Printers, 16a, Great Windmill Street, Haymarket.